DISNEY'S

102 DALMATIANS

A Junior Novel Adapted by Alice Downes

D0030616

New York

First Edition
1 3 5 7 9 10 8 6 4 2

The text for this book is set in 12-point ITC Berkeley Book.
Library of Congress Catalog Card Number: 00-104556
ISBN 0-7868-4440-X

For more Disney Press fun, visit www.disneybooks.com

Chapter

Mr. Torte was sleek and he was sly. He was an expensive London lawyer who had been summoned to the Behaviour Control Unit on behalf of one of his clients.

"My client is not a laboratory animal, Dr. Pavlov," said Mr. Torte.

"Your client wants out of prison, Mr. Torte," replied Dr. Pavlov. He led the lawyer to a corridor of locked rooms, each with an observation window. Mr. Torte peered into the first room, his eyes narrowing suspiciously. He saw a brightly colored canary perched happily on the head of a peaceful cat.

Dr. Pavlov explained. "I've patented a humane cocktail of electric shock treatment, aversion therapy, hypnosis, drugs, and plenty of green vegetables."

Mr. Torte moved on to the second door. He looked inside and saw a fox grinning calmly as it watched a plump goose splash in a tub.

He turned quickly to door number three. Behind it was a sharp-toothed mongrel cuddling with a rabbit.

Dr. Pavlov continued. "But, of course, the real challenge remained. I mean, this is a prison, not a pet shop."

"And I don't represent animals in court," said Mr. Torte irritably. "My client is . . ."

"Cured!" Dr. Pavlov broke in.

Mr. Torte looked inside the next observation window and gasped in surprise. There was his client, the infamous puppynapper herself, Cruella De Vil. And she was surrounded by Dalmatians!

Cruella's wild black and white locks had been tamed into a stylishly smooth hairdo. Her once wicked eyes twinkled merrily as she stroked and cuddled the spotted dogs.

Mr. Torte looked on in amazement at what Dr. Pavlov's behavior control therapy had accomplished. "Brush up on your Swedish, Dr. Pavlov," he told the scientist. "This could be your Nobel Prize."

It wasn't long before Mr. Torte and his client had their day in court. An audience of dog lovers looked on worriedly.

Mr. Torte faced the judge: "My client, who just three years ago would think nothing of emptying a row of kennels for the makings of a winter coat, who dognapped her way all over London for her spring collection . . ."

"Do get on with it, Mr. Torte," the judge interrupted.

"M'lord, thanks to the miraculous therapy of Dr. Pavlov," the lawyer continued, "my client is now someone who not only loves dogs and all our furry friends with a sentimental passion, but actually has an aversion to fur just this side of barking mad."

"Thank you, Mr. Torte," said the judge. He turned his attention to Cruella. "Cruella De Vil . . ."

Cruella interrupted. "Do call me Ella. Cruella sounds so . . . cruel."

"Ms. De Vil," said the judge, "I am releasing you to the custody of the Probation Department. You will perform five hundred hours of community service. . . ."

The court exploded in an uproar. Animal lovers and their pets booed, growled, stomped their feet, and pounded their paws. "ORDER! ORDER!" cried the judge. "If I hear one more bark, I'll muzzle every one of you." He turned to Mr. Torte. "Your client is a wealthy woman, I believe," he said thoughtfully.

"After my exorbitant fees," answered Mr. Torte, "her assets will be a mere eight million pounds, my lord."

The judge turned to Cruella. "Then you are bound to keep the peace to the sum of eight million pounds. If forfeited, the money will be donated forthwith and entire to the Dogs' Homes of the Borough of Westminster. Which means, if you repeat the offense, your entire fortune will go to the dogs."

Cruella smiled her newly reformed and very sweet smile. "How wonderful, my lord! You are a Solomon."

Cruella had been granted probation. She was free!

Alonso, Cruella's faithful valet, was waiting for his boss outside the prison gates. The iron gates opened slowly. Cruella swept toward him. "Alonso! My ever loyal valet, my only visitor, stuttering sweetly on the far side of the bulletproof glass. You didn't have to drive all this way. I was happy to take the bus."

Overcome with emotion, Alonso presented her with a large wrapped box. "Ms. De Vil, I've been waiting for this day and I hope I'm not being too presumptuous, but I b-brought you a gift."

"Why, Alonso . . . how considerate," said Cruella happily. She untied the bow with a delicate tug, and the top of the box flew off. Out jumped an exquisitely hairless dog. The few strands of hair on its bony head were black and white, just like Cruella's.

"H-he's a hairless breed. I thought it appropriate, considering . . ." Alonso's voice trailed off as he awaited his mistress's reaction.

Cruella lifted the dog into the air and squealed with delight. "And you were so right! I think I'll call him Fluffy."

Fluffy snarled, showing his canines.

"Look, he's smiling at me," cooed Cruella.

Back in Dr. Pavlov's laboratory, the bonging of Big Ben blared from the television. Big Ben, the large bell in the clock tower of the Houses of Parliament, was a famous London monument. The doctor's assistant stopped flipping through the television channels to listen to it mark the hour.

Suddenly, the sound of ferocious battles erupted from behind the experimental laboratory doors!

Dr. Pavlov rushed from his office and flung open one of the lab doors. The goose flapped out, pursued by a snarling fox. He opened the second door, and cried out at what he saw.

"Quick!" he called to his assistant. "Turn down the television!" The assistant hurried over to the television, while Dr. Pavlov opened the last lab door. Quietly, the cat strolled out, a few yellow feathers drifting from its whiskers.

"A unique sound pattern, very loud," Dr. Pavlov was muttering to himself.

"That were Big Ben on the telly," offered the assistant.

"Yes, it must have jolted their brainwaves back into . . ." Dr. Pavlov grabbed his assistant, shaking him angrily. "This mustn't get out," he said in menacing whisper. "Do you hear me? It never happened!"

Chapter

Big Ben was chiming through London. Chloe Simon's office was so close to its clock tower that her windows rattled with the noise.

"The dog ate your pay stub," she shouted between bongs. "Can't you do better than that?"

Chloe worked as a probation officer. Ex-convicts checked in with her weekly, promising her they wouldn't get into any more mischief.

Today she was meeting with Ewan. Tattooed where he wasn't pierced, he had recently found a job working at a local dog shelter. Chloe wanted to see his pay stubs.

"I was abducted by aliens," Ewan told her. "Plucked me out of Piccadilly, they did. It was . . ." Another enormous bong sounded. "How can you work here? I can't even keep my own story straight."

Chloe rose to shut the window and the noise lessened. "I won't say it again, Ewan," she told him wearily. "No pay stub, no probation."

Ewan searched his pockets and produced dog treats, a chew toy, and two crayons. "The dog shelter suits me," he said. "I think I've found myself." He next pulled a photo from his pocket. "Oh, here's a snap of me with the dogs."

In the photo, Ewan posed with a motley crew of dogs outside Second Chance Dog Shelter. Someone's boot was also in the photo with a brightly colored macaw sitting on it. "That's the boss," said Ewan, pointing at the boot. "He's a top bloke. You'd love him."

Finally Ewan produced a soggy slip of paper.

11

He handed Chloe the damp, disintegrating slip. "Told you. Drooler got ahold of it."

But the slip was not a pay stub. "This is an IOU!" cried Chloe.

Ewan explained. "Yes, well, we're tight on funds at the moment."

Just then, Chloe's boss, Agnes, entered the office, carrying a red folder. "Ewan was just off," Chloe said.

"Thanks, miss!" said Ewan, happy to escape. "Next week, then."

"With pay stubs," Chloe reminded him. "Or the aliens will have to pluck you out of Whitemoor Prison." She smiled at Ewan. "Am I being clear?"

"Supremely," said Ewan. "Keep the photo." He dashed past Agnes and out the door.

Before Agnes could explain what was in the red folder, the phone rang. Chloe dove for it, sending the stacks of papers on her desk flying. She held the receiver to her ear and color began to rise to her cheeks. "Stay calm," Chloe said in a very loud, not very calm voice. "I'm on my way."

Chloe ran around the office cramming papers into her briefcase. She was so laden down that Agnes had to pop the red folder into her mouth! Off she ran.

Chapter

At Second Chance Dog Shelter, playtime was just beginning and the place was already a mess. Opened, empty cages were crammed everywhere. Ragged doggie toys were scattered on the floor.

In the middle of the mayhem, Kevin Shepherd, the shelter's director, was on all fours with a rope clamped firmly between his jaws.

At the other end of rope was Drooler, a large

bullmastiff. Gobs of drool were flying from his mouth as he pulled at the rope.

A gleeful collection of strays and mutts surrounded the pair, barking their support for Drooler.

"He's pulling! Combination shake and dribble!" called Waddlesworth. A precocious macaw, Waddlesworth lived at the dog shelter because he believed he was a dog! He could not fly, because, as he often explained, "Dogs can't fly."

With a burst of strength, Kevin managed to stand, pulling Drooler toward him. Sensing his comrade's momentary weakness, a Border terrier named Chomp began nipping at Kevin's pant leg, steering him toward the opened door of a large cage.

Seeing what Chomp was up to, Digger, a borzoi, started digging coal from a bucket.

As planned, Kevin slipped on the coal and rolled into the cage, losing his end of the rope on the way. Waddlesworth pulled the pin on the cage and the door clanged shut!

The dogs roared with approval. "All's fair! All's fair in tug-of-war!" pronounced Waddlesworth.

When Ewan returned from his visit to the parole office, he found his boss locked in the cage. "That's pathetic, Kev," he said. He put down the dog food he was carrying and set Kevin free. "How many times will you fall for that one? And it can't be good for your choppers. I got a good dentist, if you need one." Ewan showed off his snaggly teeth.

"Where'd you get the dog food?" asked Kevin worriedly. "You didn't pinch it, did you?"

"Me? No, I'm done with all that," Ewan replied.

He turned to the dogs. They had lined up, holding bowls in their mouths. Ewan began pouring food while the dogs wagged their tails appreciatively.

"Save some for tomorrow," Kevin reminded him. "I don't know where our next meal's coming from."

"My mum always said when the 'art 'opes, 'ope comes knocking," offered Ewan.

"'Art 'opes'?" repeated Kevin, puzzled. A loud knock on the door interrupted his thoughts. "Hope comes knocking!"

But when Kevin opened the door, he found his landlord, Mr. Button, tacking up an eviction notice!

"You can't just turn all these dogs loose in the city!" protested Kevin. "Give us another chance."

"I'm not the one running a charity here," snapped Mr. Button. "Maybe you can get away with this nonsense in Wales, but this is England. We're civilized here."

Chomp edged toward Mr. Button and began to growl. Frightened, the landlord backed away. "Keep that monster away from—" A huge snarl from behind him made Mr. Button jump. He looked down to see Waddlesworth, puffing out his chest and doing his best German shepherd imitation.

"You and your mangy pack are out of here tomorrow!" cried Mr. Button. He stormed off.

Ewan, Waddlesworth, and the dogs were silent. "Don't worry," Kevin said softly. "Everything will be all right." He just didn't know how.

Chapter

Chloe fumbled for her keys outside her apartment. "I came as soon as you rang," she called through the door. "The traffic was beastly."

Inside the apartment, a Dalmatian charged full speed toward the door. He hit the lock and the handle with one swipe of his paw. The door opened.

"Dipstick!" Chloe called. But the dog had raced off. Chloe found him tearing strips of cloth. The floor was covered with shredded sheets.

"Good work!" cheered Chloe. "Did you remember to . . . ?" A kettle whistled in the kitchen, and Chloe smiled. "You're going to make a wonderful father."

Chloe turned to the armoire. Taking a deep breath, she opened the double doors. There, nestled in the corner and wrapped in a basket was a tired, happy, and pregnant Dalmatian.

Chloe knelt beside her. "My dear, sweet, Dottie. You look absolutely beautiful. Don't worry. Everything will be fine."

Chapter

olding Fluffy securely, Cruella De Vil swept into her mansion. "Home sweet home," she said wistfully. "It's smaller than I remember."

From the walls above, generations of De Vil ancestors, each with black and white Cruellalike tresses, stared down from their gilded frames.

"I k-kept everything just as you left it," stammered Alonso.

"Come, Fluffy. We'll share a bath," Cruella crooned as she slowly ascended the winding staircase. "An interminable soak in scalding water scented with lavender and a drop of Sumatran creosote."

For a moment, the mansion was engulfed in silence. Perhaps the ancient walls themselves were holding their breath, waiting for a glimpse of their old mistress to reemerge from the depths of this soft-spoken impostor?

A sudden scream rattled the windows. Cruella bolted from her boudoir, a look of frenzied panic on her face. Fluffy leaped from the banister, plunging into Alonso's arms.

"FUR!" Cruella's voice echoed through the house. "IT'S EVERYWHERE! Lock my furs away. Bury them beyond sight and memory!"

"I will!" Alonso jumped to the task, but stopped suddenly. "Even your Siberian borzoi boots?"

"Yes. Yes!" cried Cruella.

"Even the Mongolian pony-skin trousers and the printed donkey jacket, which are not furs, technically speaking?"

"Everything!" Cruella wailed.

"And your panda Mao jacket?"

"NOW!" Cruella screeched.

"Just checking," said Alonso. He scurried into Cruella's bedroom.

Much later, Alonso had finally dragged the last of the offending pelts down to the first floor, and thrown them into the depths of the mansion's secret room.

"That's the last of them," he told Cruella.

"And this . . ." A trembling Cruella thrust a large rolled piece of paper at him and fled.

Alonso unrolled the paper and saw a drawing. The very drawing that had caused howls around London and landed Cruella in the clink. Alonso held the drawing of the Dalmatian fur coat!

"Seal the room," called Cruella. "Quickly!"

As Alonso nailed the secret door shut, Cruella held her anxious new pet close. "Oh, Fluffy, now Mummy can start a new life."

Chapter 6

Chloe's eyes filled with tears as she lifted a newborn puppy into the sunshine.

"It's a girl," she said softly. "Welcome to the world, little one. There's someone here to see you."

Dipstick sniffed the pup, giving her ear a loving lick.

Chloe tucked the puppy against Dottie's warm belly beside her brothers. Everyone was exhausted but happy.

An odd squeaking sounded. Chloe saw that the tiny girl puppy was sucking on a rubber toy. "You're an odd one, aren't you?" she said, picking the puppy up. "You won't get much nourishment there."

Chloe kissed the top of the puppy's head and made a place for her at her mother's side.

Then she partially closed the armoire doors and slumped into an armchair. Her foot knocked a newspaper off the footstool.

Dipstick wandered over to Chloe. When he saw the paper's front page, he let out a howl.

"Dipstick, what—?" Chloe quickly saw what he was barking at. Cruella De Vil was on the front page of the paper. "CRUELLA FREED!" she read in disbelief. "How could they free that . . . that . . ." Chloe didn't have words for what Cruella was. "I pity the poor probation officer who . . ."

The words froze in Chloe's throat. She reached for the red file Agnes had thrust at her earlier. The name "Cruella De Vil" was written on the front.

"Oh, no! I refuse," Chloe cried. She pulled Dipstick close. Dipstick was one of the ninety-nine puppies that Cruella had been sent to jail for stealing. "You remember her, don't you? When I think what she would have done to you . . ." Dipstick put his paw on Chloe's arm pleadingly. He stared worriedly into her eyes.

Chloe sighed. She knew what he was asking her. "All right. I'll do it. I'll keep my eyes on her," she promised. "I'll do it for you. And for the family."

Chapter

The following morning Cruella De Vil stood in the doorway of Chloe's office.

"Ms. De Vil," said Chloe coldly. "You are five minutes late."

Cruella flicked her eyes at Big Ben, visible through Chloe's window. "Your clock's fast," she said.

Chloe ignored her remark. "I'm Chloe Simon, your probation officer," she said.

"Of course you are," Cruella purred, pulling

a chair close to Chloe's desk. "We're going to be such good friends. You're my first probation officer."

"Friends?" Chloe repeated incredulously.

"And you're going to help me be a useful member of society, aren't you?" continued Cruella. "Find me a little niche somewhere. Something with puppy dogs! Could you manage that?"

"Absolutely not!" blurted Chloe. "I see you more as a . . . coal miner. Or perhaps something in the sewers."

"I see," answered Cruella. Her glance fell on the photograph that Ewan had given Chloe. Cruella read the words SECOND CHANCE DOG SHELTER.

Cruella smiled. "Must dash," she said perkily. "I'm sure we'll get on better next time. You have such a sweet little office. I'll bring you some scatter cushions. 'Bye!"

Chloe sat open-mouthed as Cruella swished from the room. Perhaps other criminals could be reformed, but Cruella?

Chapter

"Keep your gnashers in your gobs," Ewan reminded the dogs. "This is a nonviolent protest."

The Second Chance dogs stood outside the shelter entrance holding protest signs in their mouths.

Kevin cleared his throat. "This is your last chance, Mr. Button. When the press sees what you're doing to these poor dogs, you'll be the most hated man in London."

As if on cue, a press van pulled up at top speed and screeched to a halt in front of the shelter. A frazzled crew of reporters and camera people eagerly jumped to the pavement.

"You're just in time," said Kevin happily. But the reporters were not interested in him or the shelter.

"Here she comes!" cried a reporter.

Kevin was amazed to see a luxury automobile screech to a stop in front of the shelter. "Cruella De Vil?" asked Kevin, puzzled.

Cruella swept toward him. "Please, call me Ella." She gestured at the shelter. "This place and I were made for each other. Is it yours?"

"Yes," answered Kevin.

"No, it's mine," broke in Mr. Button.

Cruella snapped her fingers and Alonso sprang forward. "Buy the dump," she ordered. With a distasteful look at Mr. Button, she added, "And give him a little extra for a new tie."

Cruella De Vil was the new owner of Second Chance Dog Shelter. All around Kevin, his animals stifled frightened whines.

30

Chapter

As soon as Chloe saw Cruella on the television taking over Second Chance, she jumped on her scooter and sped to the shelter.

Kevin and Ewan were both outside when Chloe pulled up.

"Look. Another volunteer. See, Ewan? There are good-hearted people everywhere," said Kevin. Chloe pulled off her helmet, and Kevin took his first look at her. "Beautiful, good-hearted people," he said softly.

"It's my probation officer!" Ewan said nervously.

Chloe ignored Ewan and walked up to Kevin. "You call yourself a dog lover?" she asked angrily.

"Why, yes, I do. I am!" answered Kevin, flustered.

"He does. He is," added Ewan.

Chloe flashed her ID. "I'm Chloe Simon, Cruella De Vil's probation officer."

"Is there some problem?" asked Kevin. He led Chloe into the shelter, through teams of busy construction workers.

Kevin introduced her to Waddlesworth. "Chloe, meet Waddlesworth. He's a rottweiler."

"Funny, he looks like a macaw," replied Chloe.

Waddlesworth barked loudly. "Trust me, he's a rottweiler," Kevin replied.

"I don't trust anyone who would knowingly put Cruella anywhere near dogs," said Chloe sharply. "People like Cruella don't change!"

Kevin didn't agree. "Of course they do! That's why I started Second Chance. I know what it's like to need one." Chloe tried to interrupt him, but Kevin went on. "Same goes for dogs. Chomp here chewed through three postmen before I rescued him. Now he wouldn't hurt a flea. And Digger was banned from every park in London as a menace to roses. And Drooler . . . well, Drooler hasn't changed much, but—"

"But they're dogs," Chloe said softly.

"Dogs are people, too," said Kevin. He opened a door to a back room.

Chloe gasped at the sight before her: Cruella was grooming a sheepdog with wild flourishes of hair gel.

"Hair must be a statement. A reflection of our inner life," Cruella told the uneasy sheepdog.

Stunned, Chloe stepped back out of the room. She warned Kevin, "I'll be keeping my eye on her."

"I hope so," said Kevin.

Over the next few weeks, Second Chance Dog Shelter was transformed. If Cruella wasn't in residence—cleaning and decorating and trying to coax the dogs into playing with her—she was out shopping for gourmet doggie treats or new drapes for the doggie lounge. She manned "adopt-a-pet" booths. She was on the cover of dog magazines like *Barker's Bazaar* and *Ideal Hound*. She appeared in advertisements with dogs, imploring, "Help me save them." Donations poured into Second Chance.

But whenever Chloe dropped by to check on her famous client, she couldn't help noticing that the dogs seemed to steer clear of their patron. More often than not they ran off whenever Cruella tried to pet them. Did they know something everyone else didn't know?

Chapter

One bright morning, Chloe brought all her dogs to the office for the first time. The puppies were just the right age to begin learning how to behave in public.

Agnes was thrilled to meet the puppies. "So, you're Domino," she said. A small domino hung from his collar. "And Little Dipper is easy because your tail is just like Daddy's. I know you're Oddball because you don't have any . . ."

"Shhhh!" interrupted Chloe gently. "I don't

want her to be sensitive about her lack of S-P-O-T-S."

"Is that normal at her age?" asked Agnes.

"Well, like everything else about her, it is a bit odd." Chloe looked at Oddball, who was busy playing with the telephone keys. "Will you take them to your office for a bit? I just end up staring at them and I'm sure you've noticed I've fallen dreadfully behind on my paperwork."

"I'd be delighted," said Agnes. "It's probably a good idea, with Ms. De Vil coming in."

Chloe froze. "Cruella?"

"She asked to change her appointment," said Agnes. "I thought you knew."

Agnes led the dogs out as Chloe angrily slammed down a folder. "Cruella De Vil. That wretched . . ."

"Philanthropist?" finished Cruella, appearing suddenly in the doorway.

Chloe was surprised. "I didn't realize . . ."

"Please, call me Ella," said Cruella. She swept into the office with an agenda in mind. "Now, you can't stop me, Chloe! It's my duty to demonstrate against a fur fashion show."

"And it's my duty to inform you that you'll go right back to prison if you break the law," replied Chloe.

"Won't you even let me heckle that wretched LePelt?" asked Cruella. "Just a teeny-weeny heckle—you know . . ." She paused. "MURDERER!"

Back in Agnes's office, Agnes played a computer game with Dipstick. Dottie, Little Dipper, and Domino watched attentively.

Oddball looked at her family. Then she looked at herself. She knew she was missing something: spots!

Across the hall, Oddball saw a repairman fixing a copy machine. He was covered with spots of copier toner.

With a determined wag of her tail, Oddball scampered into the hallway. She climbed on top of the copier—paying no attention to the open window behind her.

Happily, she began to roll back and forth in the spilled black ink. Soon she was covered with spots. Oddball barked joyfully.

Oddball's brothers heard her bark, and looked toward her. But the repairman was wearing headphones and did not hear the bark. He opened the lid on the copier, and Oddball was flung out the window!

Luckily, Oddball landed in a gutter just under the window ledge. But then the gutter came loose and swung away from the wall! As Oddball clung to the gutter, her brothers climbed out to rescue her.

It was Cruella who saw the puppies first.

"I knew LePelt in my bad old days," Cruella was telling Chloe. "You remember the white tiger I stole from the London Zoo? He made the coat." Cruella broke off and began staring out the window. "I've got spots before my eyes."

Chloe looked out the window and saw the puppies. She opened the window in alarm. And just then . . . Big Ben began to chime the hour.

BONG!

BONG!

BONG!

Chloe dove out on the ledge, pulling Little

38

Dipper and Domino back inside. But she could not quite reach Oddball.

When Agnes ran into the office with Dottie and Dipstick, Chloe instructed her, "Grab my legs." She stretched out the window as far as she could.

The chimes of Big Ben echoed through the building, shaking the walls.

BONG!

BONG!

BONG!

"Dr. Pavlov, help!" squealed Cruella. She could feel an enormous change coming over her. The chimes continued.

BONG!

BONG!

BONG!

"GRRRRRRRRRRRR," Dipstick growled, noticing Cruella for the first time.

Cruella turned to Dipstick. "Have we met?"

Chloe just managed to pluck Oddball by the scruff of the neck and toss her gently into the room.

Oddball landed with a thud right on Cruella! Cruella's fingers caressed Oddball's soft puppy fur.

Chloe climbed back into the office, frantically checking her dogs. "Oh, Domino, Little Dipper, I'm so . . . Where's Oddball?" Chloe rushed to take Oddball from Cruella.

Strangely calm, Cruella asked, "Are these your lovely dogs?" A shock of Cruella's hair had popped straight out from her head. Dipstick began to bark a warning. Cruella turned to him. "Now I remember you! As a puppy . . ."

Cruella stood and staggered to the door. "Why don't I come back later?" she told Chloe and Agnes. "I feel a little chilly." She stumbled into the hallway.

In the hallway, she saw the copier repairman covered with spots. The paper coming out of the machine was covered in spots, too. Everywhere she looked, Cruella saw spots!

Screaming, Cruella hurtled toward the exit. But outside, even Alonso looked spotted to her. Her car was spotted. Every building on the street was spotted. And every person, too.

Alonso was worried about his boss. "Wouldn't you be more comfortable in the car. Ms. De Vil? Ella?"

Cruella turned to Alonso. Her hair was its old explosion of black and white. "Ella's gone," she said, "and CRUELLA'S BACK!"

Cruella could not get back to her mansion fast enough—back to her furs.

"I need my furs!" she shouted. "NOW!"

Alonso frantically tried to undo the barriers to the secret fur room, but he was too slow for Cruella.

She yanked him aside. "Stand aside, worm," she snarled. She plunged her fingernails into the wood. She clung to the door like a rock climber and ripped the boards free with her bare hands!

She plunged into the room full of her furs, crying, "At last! Forgive me for abandoning you."

Then the famous drawing caught her eye. Under the eerie shadows cast by a swinging lightbulb, there it was: the design for the Dalmatian puppy coat.

"My Dalmatian puppy coat! The Coat of Dreams! The ultimate fur coat that was denied me by that canine cabal . . . for which I lost three years of my life!" cried Cruella. "Alonso, we are going to make them pay."

"How much?" asked Alonso, not fully understanding her.

"'Dipstick,' she called him," continued Cruella. "What fiendish justice! He escaped me, but I shall wreak my vengeance on the next generation."

"Sounds . . . wonderful," offered Alonso uncertainly.

"Alonso, I need you."

"I am yours," Alonso replied, trembling.

"Furnish yourself with a torch, a large

sack, and rubber-soled shoes," she ordered. "Meanwhile, I need a furrier, and I know just where to find him."

Cruella De Vil was back—and the Dalmatian puppies of London were in terrible danger!

Chapter

12

It was fashion week in London, the busiest week of year for the Greater London Animal Defense League. Tonight they were stationed outside of the fashion show given by the infamous fur designer Jean-Pierre LePelt.

Inside, runway models displayed fur bikinis, fur pajamas, fur shoes, and even fur sunglasses.

Disguised behind a black veil, Cruella swallowed a dismissive laugh. "No one is buying sable wedding dresses this season," she sneered. "Now, in polar bear—*that* would be a gown."

The music rose into a deafening crescendo and LePelt himself appeared on the runway. He was draped in his signature full-length sable trench coat. When he reached the end of the stage, he flung open his coat. The audience gasped at LePelt's shaggy tank top and fur boxer shorts.

"Fur is then, now, and forever!" he cried. "LePelt is fur!"

As LePelt spread his arms wide to bask in the expected adulation, red paint splattered across his chest. The animal rights demonstrators had stormed the show. "Animal killer!" they cried.

Raising his fist defiantly, LePelt yelled, "Fur is a natural fiber!" and stormed off the stage.

Cruella crept backstage through the chaotic crowd.

In his private dressing room LePelt was in an uncontrollable rage. "They have no *chic*," he stormed at his panicked assistants. "And LePelt is full of *chic*!"

When a knock sounded at the door, LePelt opened it, screamed, "Not here!" and slammed it shut.

Then he realized who his visitor was.

He threw open the door. "Forgive me," he said to Cruella. "My idiots did not recognize you."

"Get out!" he barked at his assistants. "You are unfit to look upon this goddess of fashion." The assistants happily fled. "Cruella, my idol, my inspiration, my joy, at my show! I'm so sorry about the demonstrators." He bowed before her.

Cruella smiled. "Demonstrators? I thought they were critics."

Her mood changed when Alonso burst into the room carrying a wriggling sack. "Here I am, Ms. De Vil."

"Who are you, little man?" asked LePelt, with a sneer. "And what are you doing in my *chambre*?"

Cruella was furious with Alonso. "Don't bring them here, you silly little cabbage!" She made Alonso sit down.

Cruella turned to LePelt. "Your reputation is

molting, darling. I am proposing an alliance between Maison LePelt and the House of De Vil."

LePelt was interested. "A merger . . . ?"

"Think of it as foreign aid," said Cruella. A small bark was heard from Alonso's bag.

"A coat . . . from *poopies*?" asked LePelt.

"Not just *poopies*," said Cruella. She cued Alonso, who brought forth a wriggling Dalmatian puppy. "*Poopies* with spots."

Chapter

Chloe did not know that her Dalmatian pups were in danger. She happily took them to the park to watch a puppet show.

Approaching the ticket booth, she heard: "One adult, three dogs, and one bird." Then she heard a strange bark, and the man corrected himself. "Four dogs, please."

It could only be Kevin. He was out with Digger, Drooler, Chomp, and Waddlesworth.

Kevin was happy to see Chloe and her dogs.

"Are these your Dalmatians?" he asked excitedly.

Chloe introduced Dipstick, Dottie, Domino, Little Dipper, and Oddball.

Oddball was fascinated by Waddlesworth. She barked at him. When Waddlesworth barked back, Oddball hid behind Chloe's legs.

"Oddball, he won't hurt you," Chloe said soothingly.

"Not unless you're a postman," Kevin joked. Then he pocketed his change from the ticket seller without counting it.

"Don't you count your change?" asked Chloe.

"Why would I?" asked Kevin.

Now Chloe knew why Kevin trusted Cruella. He trusted everyone!

Chloe bought her tickets, and everyone headed for their seats. The dogs loved the puppets' silly antics. Oddball sat up when she saw a puppet in a polka-dot sweater.

"Oh, dear," said Chloe to herself.

"What is it?" whispered Kevin.

"Oddball is obsessed with S-P-O-T-S," explained Chloe.

50

"Spots?" asked Waddlesworth. Chloe shushed him.

Suddenly, Oddball dashed onto the stage! One puppet was hitting the polka-dotted puppet. Oddball grabbed the spotted puppet in her teeth, and tried to pull it to safety. The puppet came off the puppeteer's hand. Oddball took off with the puppet in her mouth!

Kevin, Chloe, Waddlesworth, and the dogs ran after Oddball. Outside the puppet theater, the group saw a balloon seller struggling to his feet. Above him, a clump of balloons floated away—with Oddball tangled in the strings!

Kevin and Chloe tried to grab Oddball, but she floated out of reach.

Kevin turned to Waddlesworth. "Now's the time. You can save that puppy's life. All you have to do is fly up there and snip a few strings."

"Not all of them," added Chloe worriedly.

"Right," agreed Kevin. "Just a few. Until she starts to float down. You can do it! Fly!"

Waddlesworth hopped from Kevin's shoulder—and dropped like a stone. "Dogs can't fly! Can't fly," he squawked.

Now the balloons had drifted over the puppet theater. Kevin clambered onto the roof of the theater, and jumped for the trailing balloon strings. He caught them! Kevin, Oddball, and the balloons began to fall.

Chloe, Waddlesworth, and the dogs hurried around the theater to see what had happened. They found Kevin sitting atop a playground slide with Oddball and the puppet tucked securely under his arm.

Kevin slid down the slide to meet Chloe. He handed her Oddball.

"I don't know how to thank you," Chloe told Kevin.

Imitating Kevin's voice, Waddlesworth piped up: " How 'bout dinner?"

"I beg your pardon?" asked Chloe.

Kevin glared at Waddlesworth, but decided to plunge ahead. "I was inviting you to dinner," said Kevin.

"Dinner would be lovely," said Chloe. The dogs thought so, too.

52

Chapter

Wrapped in oversized furs, Cruella and LePelt hunched over the design of the puppy coat.

"I need a special place, for three special puppies," said Cruella. Drawing feverishly, she added a hood to the coat.

Alonso entered the room proudly. "F-forty Dalmatian puppies shipped off to P-Paris." He nodded at LePelt. "To his shop."

Cruella's forgotten Fluffy peeked out from under the sofa. No one noticed him, or his look of worry.

"Not enough," said LePelt.

"We need one hundred and two," announced Cruella. "This time I want a *hooded* spotted puppy coat."

"It's not that easy to steal all those . . ." began Alonso.

"Steal? Who said anything about stealing?" interrupted LePelt.

"What did you think, LePelt?" asked Cruella coldly. "That we'd have time to breed them?"

"Skinning is one thing, but stealing . . ." protested LePelt.

"Stop whining!" barked Cruella. "I have a perfectly good idiot to take the fall."

LePelt looked at Alfonso. He had never liked Cruella's assistant and was happy to think of him in prison. But Cruella had not been thinking of Alfonso. Her target was someone far more innocent.

Chapter

15

Kevin was nervous when he arrived at Chloe's apartment. Chomp was carrying the video *Lady and the Tramp* in his mouth and Digger was barking impatiently.

"Get on with it!" urged Waddlesworth.

"Give me a minute!" said Kevin. "Where's my comb?" When Kevin couldn't find his comb, Drooler licked his hair to plaster it down.

"Thanks, mate," said Kevin. He summoned his courage and rang the doorbell.

Dipstick opened the door and the animals greeted each other happily. Waddlesworth even brought a gift for Oddball: the spotted sweater from the puppet show!

Oddball and Chloe were delighted. The happy pup wriggled into the sweater.

"Mr. Puppeteer and I came to an arrangement," explained Kevin.

The animals settled down to watch *Lady and the Tramp*. Kevin and Chloe went to a restaurant.

They couldn't help talking about Cruella. Chloe still did not trust her. Kevin tried to reassure Chloe. "Did you know that if Cruella ever goes back to dognapping, her millions go straight to the Dogs' Homes in the Borough of Westminster?" he asked.

"I did, because it's in her file," replied Chloe. "But how did you . . ."

"She told me," said Kevin, with a grin. "And did you know Second Chance is the only shelter in the borough?"

As he spoke, Kevin dropped pieces of bread

under the table. "Can you image what Drooler would do with eight million pounds?"

"Kevin, what are you doing with your bread?" asked Chloe.

"Force of habit, I guess," he said, embarrassed.

Chloe understood. "Yes, it seems funny to be out without them."

"Remind me not to whimper when I want more water," joked Kevin. Chloe laughed, and they both relaxed.

But later, back at Chloe's apartment, Kevin felt shy again. "I had a great time," he said quietly, as his animals gathered around him.

"Me, too," said Chloe.

"Kiss the girl!" squawked Waddlesworth loudly.

Kevin ignored the bird. He looked at Chloe. "I know you don't believe in second chances," Kevin said. "Do you believe in second dates?"

Chloe grinned. "I do, actually."

"Good. G'night, Chloe," said Kevin. With a smile, he left the apartment.

Chloe smiled, and waited. A moment later the doorbell rang. There stood Kevin grinning sheepishly. He had forgotten his pets.

Chapter

The next morning, Kevin was still thinking about his date with Chloe, when the phone rang.

"Second Chance," he answered. An unknown caller reported that some puppies had been abandoned just around the corner. Kevin wrote down the address, and sent Ewan to get them.

"Abandoned no more," said Ewan confidently. As Ewan hurried out the back door, he failed to notice Alonso hiding nearby, carrying a writing sack of Dalmatian puppies!

Soon after Ewan left, Kevin heard Waddlesworth squawk, "The coppers!"

A police car pulled up to the shelter. Kevin stepped outside to greet the police. "How can I help you, officer?"

An officer presented him with a warrant. They were going to search the premises.

Kevin followed the police into the shelter. "What's all this about?" he asked.

"Sixteen Dalmatian puppies were reported stolen last night," explained an officer.

Moments later another officer appeared carrying a sack. He reached in and held up a wriggling Dalmatian puppy.

Kevin was pleading his innocence just as Chloe and Cruella arrived.

Chloe could not believe the police were accusing Kevin of stealing Dalmatians. "He's not the one!" she cried. She pointed at Cruella. "She is! Why suspect Kevin?"

"Caught him red-handed. And he's got a record for dognapping," said the officer.

Kevin jumped in. "I can explain . . ."

"You can explain where you were last night," said an officer.

"I was . . . out," said Kevin.

"He was out with me!" blurted Chloe.

Suddenly Ewan arrived. "Here's the puppies you asked me to grab, boss." He carried a cardboard box full of Dalmatian pups.

Chloe was stunned.

"Why would I steal Dalmatians?" cried Kevin. "What motive could I possibly—"

"The judge's order!" interrupted Cruella. "Kevin, how could you?" She turned to the police. "If I'm caught stealing puppies, my entire fortune goes to him," she explained. "Would that be a motive?"

Chloe watched in disbelief as the paddy wagon pulled away carrying Kevin—and Drooler, Chomp, Digger, and Waddlesworth. Kevin's animals had refused to leave his side.

Just then, Cruella put a comforting hand on Chloe's shoulder. "Don't be hard on yourself, my dear. We were both fooled."

"I'm sorry, Ms. De Vil. I had no idea Kevin was . . ." Chloe's eyes welled up with tears.

"This is all so dreadful," said Cruella. "You need distraction, darling. I'm having a few friends round for dinner tonight with their dogs. Won't you and yours join us? Adults only, of course. Remember, we have the doggies to live for."

Chapter 17

The cream of London society arrived at Cruella's mansion with their dogs in tow. The rooms filled with a vast array of finely dressed guests and their coifed and bejeweled pets.

Cruella swept over to Chloe and Dipstick. She was ablaze in a wild red gown. Dipstick growled.

"Dipstick!" scolded Chloe. "Be polite. She's changed."

Cruella smiled. "And are your little spotted puppies safe and snug at home?"

"Yes, they're with Dottie," replied Chloe.

Cruella's smile broadened. Her plan was working. She led Chloe and Dipstick to the dining room.

Dogs and people sat together at a long table overflowing with food. Fountains splashed around ice sculptures shaped like bones.

"Tonight our dogs join us at table so we can show our appreciation to a magnificent species," Cruella announced. "The future promises the most intimate of relationships between me and our furry friends. From now on, we'll be closer than ever."

When the food was served, dogs began to scramble onto the table after the delicious treats. Soon food was flying! The human guests were splattered. Tails wagged in their faces. Dogs stepped on their plates.

Amid the chaos, Dipstick heard a tiny, furtive bark. He looked down. There was Fluffy. The poor hairless creature barked softly in greeting, and looked around worriedly.

Cruella goes free!

A reformed Cruella gets a dog.
"Look, he's smiling at me," she coos.

Cruella meets Chloe, her probation officer. "Find me a little niche somewhere," Cruella says sweetly. "Something with puppy dogs."

Cruella finds a dog shelter in trouble . . .

...and she buys the whole place!

Second Chance Dog Shelter will never be the same.

Chloe does not trust Cruella.
She won't let Cruella near her precious Dalmatians.

The chimes of Big Ben undo Cruella's behavior therapy.
The cruel returns to Cruella!

Cruella meets her friend Jean-Pierre LePelt, the notorious furrier.
They are going to make a coat—a Dalmatian puppy fur coat!

Cruella steals puppies, and makes it look as though
Kevin, the owner of Second Chance, is the dognapper!

Cruella chases the Dalmatian puppies into a bakery.

Look out, puppies!

Cruella's cake is cooked. She is no match for 102 Dalmatians.

Woof!

Chloe caught sight of the pair leaving the room. She followed them out.

Back at Chloe's apartment, another part of Cruella's plan was falling into place.

LePelt sneaked in through a window, with a puppynapping sack. Turning on his flashlight, LePelt crept toward the puppies. "Ah, *bon soir*, my little ones," he said. "I am the great LePelt and you are, 'ow you say? 'Dog meat.'"

But before he could touch a single puppy, Dottie charged! Little Dipper and Domino ran toward the front door. Oddball scampered to the window, sounding the Twilight Bark: an all-dog alert.

Then Oddball felt LePelt's hand lifting her up by her spotted sweater. Again, Dottie charged to the rescue. But this time, LePelt snapped the sack over her head. With their mother captured, the three small puppies didn't have a chance to escape LePelt.

Meanwhile, Fluffy led Dipstick and Chloe to a

low-hanging portrait of a particularly gruesome De Vil ancestor. Fluffy flicked a switch. The portrait swung forward, revealing a door.

Dipstick opened the door. He began barking angrily. Chloe gasped. Amid an outrageous assortment of furs was a drawing of the Dalmatian puppy coat!

Now a faint barking reached Dipstick's ears. It was the Twilight Bark. Puppies across London had passed on Oddball's alarm. Dipstick raced off. He had to find his family. Fluffy left the room right behind him.

"Dipstick!" called Chloe. "Where are you . . ." She broke off when she saw Cruella standing in the doorway.

"Surprise!" crowed Cruella. "Earlier than I'd planned, but *c'est la vie.*"

"I hereby revoke your probation," said Chloe angrily.

Cruella laughed. "And I hereby lock you up, darling. Because with St. Kevin of Assisi in the clink, it wouldn't look good if three *more* puppies were reported missing!"

Chloe went pale. She knew who those three puppies were—Little Dipper, Domino, and Oddball.

"Good-bye my dear," said Cruella. "I'll think of you every time I wear your sweet little dogs." She slammed the door shut and locked it.

The Twilight Bark was passed all the way to the prison. Huddled with Kevin on his cot, the dogs listened closely. They whimpered with concern.

Waddlesworth translated for Kevin. "Tubble, there's tubble!" he squawked.

"Tubble?" said Kevin. "Oh, 'trouble.' Must be puppies talking."

"Widdow ones. Bad man gwab widdow ones," continued Waddlesworth. "Twee potted doggies."

"Bad man grabs three little spotted doggies," said Kevin. "Oh, no! Chloe's dogs!"

The dogs barked in confirmation.

"We have to get out of here!" said Kevin firmly.

Waddlesworth knew what he had to do. He

slipped through the cell bars, and walked toward the sleepy guard. Crooning a lullaby, Waddlesworth made the guard fall asleep. Then he lifted the keys, and waddled back to the cell with them.

Chloe was trying to escape, as well. She pulled a closet pole free from a pile of furs. Furiously, she battered and pried at the door.

Then she charged at the door. Just before she got there, it swung open! Chloe tumbled down the stairs.

Dazed, she looked up to see that Fluffy had set her free. The tiny dog had jumped on a chair cushion and reached the latch.

Chloe leaped to her feet. She had to get home.

Kevin and Chloe arrived at her apartment within seconds of each other.

They were too late. All the furniture was scattered topsy-turvy, and the pillows had been split open. Books lay ripped and torn all over the carpet.

"They're gone!" cried Chloe. Dottie, Little Dipper, Domino, and Oddball were not there. Chloe did not know where Dipstick was either.

"Kevin, I'm so sorry," Chloe apologized miserably. "I should have trusted you."

"No, I never should have trusted Cruella," said Kevin. "And with my police record . . ." Kevin had to explain about his dognapping conviction. "I broke into a lab and freed the dogs. They were using them for experiments."

"*That* was your dognapping conviction?" Chloe hugged him. "Oh, Kevin!"

Meanwhile, Drooler had been sniffing near the couch. At his woof, Digger ran over and started digging, sending magazines shooting across the floor. Chomp plucked something from the pile, and brought it to Kevin.

"Something rotten in Denmark! Rotten in Denmark!" squawked Waddlesworth.

Kevin and Chloe looked down at a train ticket. LePelt must have lost it in his struggle with the dogs. Chloe read the ticket. "Paris . . . the Orient Express at ten. We can just make it!"

Chapter

In an alley near St. Pancras Station, Cruella was eager to see the puppies LePelt had stolen. She approached his truck.

"Where are they?" she whispered.

LePelt lifted the canvas cover off the truck—and Dipstick rushed out, teeth bared. The dog had made it back to Chloe's apartment, just as the furrier had been pulling away.

LePelt and Alonso began to flee in terror, but Cruella coolly whipped off a long strand of pearls and lassoed Dipstick before he could bite LePelt. Dipstick was locked in the crate with Dottie.

Now Cruella could finally get her hands on the puppies. "Oh, yes!" she cried, lifting them from the sack. "Oh, LePelt, I know you understand now. The spotted sweetness . . ."

"What about them?" said LePelt, nodding toward the adult dogs.

"Too coarse," sneered Cruella. "But they'll make a lovely carpet for my car."

Cruella's glee turned to horror when she peeled back Oddball's spotted sweater. "A RAT!" shrieked Cruella, dropping the pup. "I asked for spotted dogs, and you brought me a white rat!"

Oddball scurried off. "Alonso!" cried Cruella. "Find the dog. Kill it. LePelt and I will be on the Orient Express."

"Kill?" repeated Alonso worriedly.

"The last time I underestimated a puppy, I wound up in the pokey," said Cruella. She and LePelt headed toward the Orient Express.

71

Alonso scanned the train station; finally he saw the little pup. But Oddball was too quick and clever to be caught. Alonso gave up. He had a train to catch.

Chapter

Chloe, Kevin, the dogs, and Waddlesworth dashed into the train station and searched frantically for the Orient Express.

From across the tracks, they saw Cruella in one of the luxury train compartments. She was sipping champagne and celebrating. The train was beginning to move.

Aboard the train, Cruella asked Alonso, "You took care of the rat?"

"You will never see it again," pledged Alonso.

But that little puppy was at that very moment running beside the Orient Express. Oddball had heard faint barking from inside the baggage car. Her family was aboard.

Kevin, Chloe, and Kevin's animals raced toward the Orient Express. As the train pulled out, Chloe screamed, "Oddball!"

The puppy was trying to jump onto the end of the last train car.

"Don't jump! Don't jump!" screeched Waddlesworth. The bird climbed all over Kevin's head in agitation.

"She'll be killed!" wailed Chloe.

Suddenly, Waddlesworth leaped from Kevin's head. He glided clumsily over the tracks.

"Flap your wings!" cried Kevin excitedly. "You can fly! Good dog!"

Waddlesworth began flapping as hard as he could. He soared toward Oddball. "DOGS CAN FLY!" Waddlesworth said as he swooped down on the puppy, grabbed her with his beak, and hurtled toward the open door of the last train car.

Chloe, Kevin, and the dogs watched in relief as the bird and puppy landed safely inside the train. The Orient Express picked up speed and roared away from the station.

"The Eurostar," said Chloe, remembering the high-speed train to Paris. "We can still catch them!"

The next morning, the Orient Express pulled into Paris. Baggage workers loaded the crate filled with dogs into one of LePelt's trucks.

"Careful!" chided Alonso. "Mustn't harm the '*poopies*.'" The frightened puppies barked as loudly as they could.

When Chloe, Kevin, and his animals arrived in Paris, there was no sight (or sound) of Cruella or the stolen pups. The group did not know where to look first.

Digger howled loudly. Nearby, a Parisian bulldog heard Digger's howl and barked a response. The bulldog had heard the puppies' cries. He could set the group on Cruella's trail.

Kevin watched his dogs communicate with

their new friend. "I didn't know you spoke French," said Kevin. Then he realized, "Of course, you speak dog!"

Jumping into a cab, the group followed a trail of barks and woofs from helpful French dogs that had heard the puppies' frantic calls. The dogs led them right to LePelt's workshop.

Chapter

20

Inside LePelt's illegal Parisian sweatshop, hundreds of workers slaved feverishly away at their sewing machines. The workers were too frightened of LePelt to look anywhere but at their work.

No one noticed Waddlesworth and Oddball sneak in the door behind Cruella and LePelt. The brave pair had hidden in Cruella's car, and followed her into the workshop.

Waddlesworth noticed a small hole in the

floor. Through the hole, he looked down on a dank cellar teeming with the trapped Dalmatian pups. He nudged Oddball to take a look.

Waddlesworth began to tear at the floor with his beak, trying to make the hole bigger.

Outside, Kevin lifted the chute door that led to the cellar. He could hear the puppies whimpering below.

Sliding down the chute, Kevin landed in the center of the basement room. The captive dogs dove on him, licking his face with joy.

Down the chute scooted Chloe, Chomp, Digger, and Drooler.

Amid the happy reunion, Kevin, Chloe, and the dogs did not notice the shaft of light that spilled behind them.

"Aren't you in a tight SPOT!" The sudden sound of Cruella's shrill voice sent shivers scrambling down the puppies' spines. She was peering down from the chute entrance above. "What fun to get away with murder!" she howled, slamming the chute door and locking it.

"There must be some way out of here," Chloe

was saying just as Waddlesworth's head poked through the hole in the low-hanging ceiling. Oddball's nose popped through the hole next, and Chloe reached up to receive Oddball's happy lick.

Chloe and Kevin quickly began lifting the puppies up and squeezing them gently through the hole. On the other side, Oddball pointed the puppies toward hiding places among the furs.

Soon the puppies were free from the cellar. But Kevin, Chloe, and the adult dogs were too big to fit through the hole. Waddlesworth worked frantically to make the escape hole larger—before Cruella returned.

Chapter 21

Back in LePelt's office, Alonso watched LePelt sharpen his revolting collection of skinning knives. Alonso was surprised to discover that the thought of the little puppies being skinned was making him feel sick.

But Cruella was giddy with glee. "The mark of a great furrier is that he does his own strangling," she enthused.

At that moment, Alonso saw a puppy run upstairs. The puppies were escaping! Alonso said nothing.

Cruella's nose twitched. She sniffed the air.

"No!" she yelled, pointing to a puppy scrambling up the stairs of the workshop. Then she saw a line of puppies hurrying up the stairs. Oddball led the puppies.

"It's the little rat!" she cried. She whirled around and faced Alonso. "You lied to me."

"Me? Why would I—?" began Alonso.

"Does she look dead to you?" said Cruella. "How do you explain that?"

"A miracle?" he offered lamely.

"You worm! I'll kill her myself!" said Cruella, storming out.

LePelt exploded with laughter. "You are a wormy little man!"

In a rage, Alonso reached for one of LePelt's skinning knives—but the one he pulled out was only an inch long.

LePelt laughed. Alonso threw the knife aside and charged the furrier. The two careened out of the office, locked in combat.

Cruella spared Alonso and LePelt a look. "You are BOTH idiots," she snarled. Then she continued up the stairs after the puppies.

When LePelt reached for Alonso, the smaller man grabbed LePelt's drooping sleeve and yanked it.

LePelt toppled onto a sewing table. The worker didn't stop his machine. LePelt's right sleeve was sewn onto the back of his coat. LePelt stumbled to his feet. Alonso flipped the stunned furrier onto another sewing table and that worker finished the job with a quick zip. LePelt's jacket was transformed into a straight-jacket!

Like an angry bear, LePelt rushed at Alonso. Alonso just slipped out of the way as LePelt's leg crashed through Waddlesworth's hole.

Chomp looked at the leg dangling in front of his face. He bared his teeth.

Struggling to pull his leg free, LePelt wound up crashing through the floor all the way to his waist. Now both of his legs hung temptingly before Chomp.

With a growl, Chomp chomped.

Above, LePelt opened his mouth to scream.

Alonso grabbed a fur muff and crammed it between LePelt's teeth.

"Who's the little man now?" asked Alonso. The surrounding workers erupted into cheers.

Alonso was transformed! He threw open the doors to the basement and freed Kevin and Chloe. "Quickly!" he called to them.

Kevin looked at Chloe. "Can we trust him?" he asked her under his breath.

"This is no time to count your change, Kevin," Chloe answered. She grabbed Alonso's arm and let him help her out of the chute.

"Upstairs," Alonso said. "She's after the puppies."

Chloe ran off in pursuit. "Call the *gendarmes*!" she shouted.

Chapter

Oddball and the other one hundred and one puppies had continued their climb up the stairs. At the top were a landing and an open window. Puppy after puppy escaped through the window onto a narrow bridge.

The bridge joined LePelt's building to the bakery next door and rose precariously over an ancient, sludge-filled Parisian canal.

A huge fan turned slowly in the wall of the bakery. Oddball woofed a signal to each puppy, telling them when the time was right to jump through the blades.

Suddenly, Cruella crashed through the window and onto the bridge!

"I'll wear you on my sleeve!" she screamed at Oddball, who hurried the last puppy through the fan and then jumped through herself.

One by one, the puppies leaped onto a metal catwalk that encircled the old industrial bakery. They scampered down stairs, and slid down pipes, desperately trying to elude Cruella.

Cruella stopped the bakery fan with her bare hands and stepped through. Her voice echoed through the building, "I'm back! And this time it's personal!"

Cruella lunged at Oddball, losing her balance. She managed to grab a dangling cable and went swinging over the bakery machinery below. As she picked up speed, her foot accidentally hit an ON button at the end of the cable.

The bakery machinery whirled into motion. Conveyor belts started rolling. Lights started flashing. The huge oven sparked to life. Flames shot out of its center.

Watching from above, Oddball saw Cruella shimmy down the cable and drop into an industrial-size mixing pan.

Cruella threw herself over the side of the mixing bowl and landed on a moving conveyor belt. Her legs shot out from under her and she grabbed on to a metal handle to save her fall. Instead, she released hundreds of eggs, which splattered on top of her! She slid down the conveyor and was flipped into a giant mixing vat.

Oddball barked to the other puppies. The puppies began pushing sacks of flour into the vat on top of Cruella. White clouds exploded around her.

As the cascading waves of flour covered all of the puppies in a coat of white, Oddball barked joyfully. Now all of the puppies looked just like her!

Next Oddball barked an order to her brothers, and they jumped onto a gleaming metal lever. A wave of milk squirted at Cruella!

Giant metallic mixing arms began to slowly descend from the ceiling. When they reached the mixing bowl, the mixing arms churned it back and forth until it formed into a huge roll of dough with Cruella at its center.

The bowl tipped, dumping the blob onto a table. Summoning all her evil strength, Cruella exploded out of the blob. She grasped the milk nozzle between her sticky hands and aimed it at the puppies, washing the flour off of them.

"Where are you?" she screamed, looking around for the one true spotless puppy. She aimed the milk straight at Oddball. The full force of the shooting milk knocked Oddball off-balance.

Sensing victory, Cruella reached out and grabbed the spotless little puppy by the neck. "Got you now," she whispered.

Suddenly the roller arm tripped, knocking Cruella back onto the table. Oddball had landed near Cruella's head. When Cruella looked up, she saw two slicing blades starting to descend.

Cruella scrambled through the slicer just

before the blades started chopping. She looked at the twin blades, then at Oddball.

"Without spots you're just not worth the trouble," she said coldly. She grabbed Oddball and threw the puppy into the slicer.

Chloe, Kevin, Waddlesworth, and the other dogs had just entered the bakery and they looked down in horror at the scene below. The puppies froze. Cruella stumbled to her feet, glowering victoriously. "And now I have to round up my coat!"

A tiny bark stopped Cruella. She turned to watch Oddball pop up from between the blades of the slicer!

Cruella's face contorted in fury. But just as she started toward the puppy, Waddlesworth swooped down from the rafters, knocking Cruella off balance and into a wedding-cake pan.

"Dogs can fly!" Waddlesworth whooped.

Cruella, ensconced in flour and goo, rolled into the fiery depths of the oven!

As the sound of sirens approached, Dottie,

Dipstick, and their puppies jumped all over each other with joy.

Dipper and Chomp began to bark. From the opposite end of the oven emerged an incredible Cruella cake. Cruella was cooked!

The puppies squirted icing at the cake. Digger shoveled on sprinkles. Chomp, of course, took a bite, revealing Cruella's leg within.

Drooler leaped up and as Cruella looked at him with dread, the dog let a pendulous glob of saliva swell above her.

"No!" wailed Cruella hoarsely.

The saliva broke free and landed on her head. Oddball dropped a wedding-cake topper onto Cruella. The topper adhered to Drooler's drool.

Then the cake dropped onto a utility cart, and with a shove from Chomp, was pushed through the double doors that separated the bakery from its pastry shop.

Cake and cart hurtled through the pastry shop, scattering tables and chairs. When the cart hit a bump, the Cruella cake went flying into the display window.

The police arrived in time to see Cruella crash into the window, with her face squished against the glass. The police carried her to a paddy wagon, where LePelt was already waiting.

One hundred and two Dalmatian puppies barked with delight.

Chapter

23

Kevin and Chloe stood arm in arm in front of Second Chance Dog Shelter. A huge cloth draped the building.

Ewan stood ready, holding on to a rope, waiting for his cue.

Kevin yelled, "Go!"

Ewan tugged at the rope. The cloth fell away, revealing a metallic sculpture of a dog's head on the shelter's roof. At the back of the building a shiny metal dog's tail climbed toward the sky. The entire building looked like a huge, metal dog.

Suddenly, Cruella De Vil's luxurious car careened to a noisy stop directly in front of the building.

"It can't be . . ." said Kevin worriedly.

Alonso stepped out of the car, looking refreshed and serene. Fluffy was nestled in his arms.

"Hello, all," he said, seemingly unaware of the effect he was having on the crowd. "I've just come from Mr. Torte. I asked him if I could have the pleasure of delivering this." He handed Kevin an envelope. Inside was a check.

"Eight million pounds!" cried Kevin.

"Judge's orders," explained Alonso. "It's for the dogs. And for the best—unless of course, she's rehabilitated!"

A figure moving along the mouth of the huge metal dog caught Alonso's eye. "What's Oddball doing up there?" he asked.

"Oh, dear," said Chloe. Drops of oil fell from the mouth of the metal dog, spotting Oddball's white coat.

"Oddball, come down from there!" called Chloe. Oddball slid down the metal dog's face and into the air. She landed softly in Chloe's waiting arms.

"Oh, Oddball, what have you done now? asked Chloe. She rubbed at some spots along Oddball's side. One of the spots didn't come off. "This one won't come off!" Chloe said excitedly. "She's got her spots! Oddball's got her spots!"

Dottie, Dipstick, and the other dogs rushed over. Waddlesworth swooped from the sky. "S-P-O-T-S," he squawked.

Oddball barked with happiness. "Woof!"